Lizzy KUROO

Saturday's Adventure

Written and Illustrated By Jamie R. Gandy

Part One
Saturday Morning

A twinkle of sunlight through my bedroom window, the flutter and chirp of birds just outside.

"BEEP-BONK-BEEP-BONK!" goes the alarm clock... Sigh...

My name is Elizabeth Kuroo, but everyone calls me Lizzy, for short.

I crawled from my bed to the floor, the floor to the door and lurked into the hallway.

With the appearance of a slobbering ghoul, and the hair of a night beast, my stomach grumbled and growled.

As I made my way into the kitchen, expecting to hear the predictably chipper call from my mom.

"Good morning!"

Followed by the sarcastic bellow of my dad.

" SHE'S ALIVE!"

But no one was to be found.

"Breakfast alone, that's different." I thought.

I plopped down at the kitchen table, with my extra big bowl of Frosted Fruity Crunchy O's. It was shaping up to be a good day.

Until...

Broom!

I remembered, Saturday= yard work day.

"**YAY!**" not really. I am not a fan, but where I live in the "burbs" as people like to say, EVERY Saturday is yard work day.

It's like a COMPETITION!

Everyone just talks about grass seed and hedge trimmers.

BLAH-BLAH-BLAH!

My mom signaled to me from the backyard in extra high spirits.

"Come outside! It's a beautiful day!" she enticed.

Ummm, no way, no how, not me. It was Saturday, a day of relaxing, a day of reading, a day of lying around on the sofa watching TV until dinner time.

"IT'S SATURDAY!" I thought. "Why can't we do yard work on Monday, or Thursday?! Do we really even need to do yard work?"

10

To escape the "Come outside!" yard work trap,
I decided to investigate the rest of the neighborhood.
Making my way through the living-room I opened the
front door.

It was as I expected. The rumble and roar of
lawnmowers surrounded me, the pungent smell of freshly
chopped grass hit me like a dodge ball in the nose.
Hedges were being hedged everywhere.

SNIP-SNIP-SNIP!

Oh the HORROR! I looked from house to house at the
neighbors working in their yards all dripping in sweat.
Eeeew!

ARGGH!

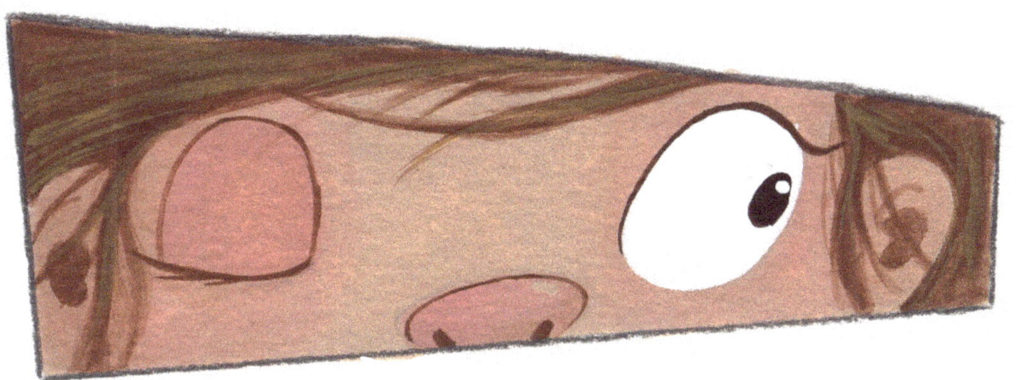

Then, from the corner of my eye, at the way far end of my street it appeared. A shining glory cast in golden morning light, an escape from a day of hiding in the bathroom and dodging hedge clippings pick-up duty.

Which in my opinion is a horrible way to spend a Saturday.

Am I right?

No, not the dog...

THE WOODS!

AN ADVENTURE!!!

J
PB

I sprang into action to gather my supplies, all the necessary tools to endure a day in the wild suburban woodlands.

I blazed from my house like a wildcat on the African Savanna, (I watched one of those nature shows on TV last night, you know the ones).

Reaching the mailbox I slammed on the brakes, something was missing.

I forgot to change out of my pajamas...

... I will be right back...

Okay, where were we? Oh!

Back on the quest, donning my survival gear, I made my way to the end of my street. It was a breathtaking day, the cool crisp morning air chilled my cheeks as I strolled the tree-lined sidewalk.

The low growl of lawnmowers slowly began to fade as I neared the entrance of the woods.

With my head held high, my gear went **JANGLE-CLANK-JANGLE-CLANK!**

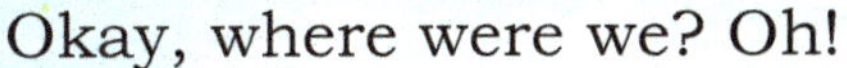

As I passed the houses, my neighbors all working in their yards stopped and stared. It was as if I had three heads!

Their eyes squinted and mouths dropped wide open. They could see the determination written on my face. I was a girl on a mission. I marched on.

JANGLE-CLANK-JANGLE-CLANK!

When I reached the entrance trail to the woods, I gazed out with the eyes of a winged predator overlooking the horizon. Hungry for adventure and ready to seize the day.

Legend has it, no one in the history of the burbs has ever ventured far from the trail.

"What are they afraid of?" I wondered.

Bears, wolves, GIANT BLOOD SUCKING SPIDERS!

Who could say?

With a deep breath, I put one foot in front of the other and didn't look back.

I trudged through the high grasses, skipped over fallen trees, leaves crunched under my feet. I hopped past razor sharp rocks and slippery stones.

I climbed over massive hills.

And tumbled down treacherous valleys. No feat was too great, no threat unnerving.

Nothing was going to stand in my way.

Part Two
Friends In Nature

The trail ahead lead me between two large boulders. There seemed to be no other way around them. As I made my way down the trail, the boulders grew closer, and closer, casting a menacing shadow, turning brilliant sunlight into what seemed like dusk. But I had no intention of turning back.

When I reached the tightest squeeze, high above I could hear a **TUMP, BUMP, THUMP,** growing closer.

Tump!
Thump!
CRUSH!

Slowly appearing through a dense cloud of dust, familiar faces were in front of me.

"Belle, Ralph?!" I shouted. "Are you trying to kill me?"

"Noooo! said Ralph. "We didn't know anyone else was out here."

"I found this dead beetle up there." said Belle, staring back with a devilish grin.

Spitting dirt from my mouth, I lifted myself off the ground and began dusting myself off. My heart pounded as I stared back at them in amazement of what just happened.

So let me introduce you to my friends.

This is Ralph with his older brother James. James just got a phone for the first time, so he and Ralph don't really hangout that much anymore.

You know how brothers can be sometimes.

But that's okay, because Ralph hangs out with us more now. Ralph is the fastest runner in our school and plays all the sports.

He's pretty cool.

This is Belle (my best friend) with her little brother Patrick. Patrick is a cute, giggly guy, but he is not old enough for going on adventures yet.

Belle and I hangout all the time, she is into to dolls and dead stuff. So that's AWESOME!

I do not have any brothers or sisters, so having these guys as friends is the best.

When they are not trying to flatten me like a pancake with a giant rock, HAHA!

As it turned out, Belle and Ralph were in the woods hiding out from the dreaded yard work day too.

"My dad makes me cut the backyard and bag all the clippings, it's the worst." Ralph explained.

"Well at least you do not have to pick up dog poop!" said Belle.

"GROSS!" we all agreed.

"So, what do you guys want to do?" I asked still spitting dirt, eeew.

" I don't know." said Belle looking at her new dead bug.

"Say, what are you doing with all of that stuff in your backpack?" asked Ralph.

"Is that a machete?!" questioned Ralph and Belle.

"Yes, you never know when it might come in handy." I answered glancing at my belt.

We agreed to follow the trail and see where it led us. I opened my compass to help guide our way. We set off on a quest for adventure, leaving the neighborhood, and yard work far, far behind us.

Part Three
In This Together

Down the trail aways, Belle suddenly panicked.

"Hey wait!" she said. "Did you guys hear something?"

"Ahh, no." Ralph and I said, with a sarcastic tone.

"Do you know you have some sticks in your hair?" Ralph asked with a chuckle.

"NO, I'm serious I heard something behind us!" Belle said skittishly.

CRUNCH

RUN!

Like a cat at a clown party, we ran for our lives!

" What was it-what was it?" I questioned gasping for a breath.

" I have no idea!" Ralph muttered. "I didn't see anything. Did you?"

" No I didn't see or hear anything." I responded.

"It, was, HUGE!" huffed Belle.

Peeking through the trees, I noticed a rickety old house covered in vines and surrounded by an iron fence and overgrown brush.

"Hey look at that you guys." I said.

"CREEP-Y!" we all agreed.

"Should we go check it out?" I asked.

"Nooo WAY! Not me." Ralph objected. "Should we?"

"YES!!" Belle and I screamed.

We collected ourselves and moved in for a closer look. We walked slowly towards the old house, trying not to make a sound. I don't even think we were breathing and definitely not blinking.

...TIP-TOE-TIP-TOE...Shhhh...

ARRGHH!!

" I'm outta here!" Ralph yelled as he ran away. " I told you guys we shouldn't go over there!"

" Wait what?!" Belle followed. " Me too, wait up!"

When I realized it was just a tiny little snake, I had to laugh, Haha!

"Scaredy cats." I whispered to myself. "Wait for me guys, you don't know the way! I have the compass remember?".

I caught up to Belle pretty quickly, (she is not a very fast runner) but Ralph was nowhere insight.

Seeing as he is the fastest runner in our school (and the biggest scaredy cat) he could be anywhere really.

"Ralph! Ralph!" we called out.

When we finally found Ralph he was pointing in the direction of a small cave.

" I can hear something inside there." he whispered.

I pulled my flashlight from my backpack and clicked it on.

"Let's move in closer so we can see inside." I suggested.

Belle and Ralph grabbed whatever they could find on the ground. Ralph found a heavy stick and Belle had a rock, we were prepared for battle this time.

We snuck in a little closer, you never know about caves. You have to be cautious, out here in the wild, you could just slip in and no one would ever find you.

a voice shouted.

"Where did that guy come from?" we asked one another.

Our hearts were thumping, our hands shook. We slowly collected our things from the ground.

"Shhh. Do you guys hear that?" I asked softly.

Then at that very moment...

BATS!

Taking cover, we frantically checked our necks for any bloody bites. Belle was waving her hands wildly over her head.

"A-Are they gone?" She asked trembling.

"I-I think so." I stuttered.

We were all a little dazed from the attack.

"That was BONKERS!" Ralph shouted looking bewildered.

" How did all those bats fit in that little cave?" I asked with a chuckle.

Looking around to be sure the bats had all flown away, I noticed lying on the ground just outside the cave a strange white stick.

" What is that?" I wondered to myself.

" Hey! Do you guys see that?" I asked.

We dusted ourselves off and cautiously walked over
to examine the suspicious white stick. I picked it up from
the ground...

"A bone..." I whispered.

"I am not touching that thing!" said Ralph.

"That's one big bone!" Belle gasped.

Looking over at Belle, "Hey those bats got those sticks
out of your hair!" Ralph giggled.

Thinking aloud. "But what type of bone is it?"
I wondered.

"Maybe it's a chicken bone?" Belle suggested.

"That's one big chicken. Maybe it's a cow bone?"
blurted Ralph.

"This is no cow's bone." I doubted.

Part Four
The Search

"Guys!!" I shouted. " I think it's a dinosaur bone!"

"Whaaaat, no way!" said Ralph.

"Wait, what?" questioned Belle. "Are you sure?"

"Yeah, I think so." I said. "Look at how big it is, it's huge!"

"Whooooa." we all said.

"Wow. What are we going to do with it?" Ralph asked.

"Find out if there are anymore." I responded boldly.

As I walked away.

"DINOSAURS!!" said Belle and Ralph.

So we set off in search for more clues.

We left no stone unturned.

We looked in holes.

We even climbed trees.

We came to a giant mound.

So we climbed it...

...And almost got run over...

We came upon what seemed to be an impassable obstacle. Standing before us was a fortress of vines.

Vines so thick we could not see past them.

With a mighty grip, I pulled my machete from my side.
I began to chop our way in with the fury of a blazing fire.
The vines could not with-stand my wrath, they swung
this way and that.

Bits and pieces of the woody foliage flung wildly past
my head.

"Stay close!" I shouted.

We trudged through ankle deep mud and vines as sharp as razors. The bugs were eating us alive, and tearing us limb from limb!

"Ouch, I got a splinter!" Belle cried out in agony.

"Hold on tight, I can see light up ahead, there must be a clearing!" I yelled back.

The mud was so thick we could hardly lift our legs.

"OH NO!" Ralph cried out. " My foot is stuck."

Looking back at Ralph I realized he was in extreme peril. An army of insects began to swarm around him.

"Give me your hand!" I encouraged.

Grabbing hold of Ralph's hand tightly I snatched him free faster than...this one time I was making popcorn on the stove and it got sooo hot, so my mom...

Forget that!

Ralph's foot popped free with a loud squishy, sucking sound. The extra weight of pulling Ralph and Belle behind me, felt like I weighed a million pounds, we were all beginning to sink. Our feet slipped and slid in the mud in every direction.

We could now see the clearing right in front of us.

Finally breaking through the thick brush.

"WE MADE IT!" we shouted triumphantly, standing proud of our great achievement. We had conquered the wilds of the suburban woodlands and lived to tell the tale...you have been reading it, so obviously we didn't die.

We were covered from head to toe in leaves and mud, plus one splinter, minus one shoe.

We had survived mysterious unknown sounds, vicious snakes, one sneaky jogger, a bat attack and a really close call with a car.

We were tired, hungry, and awfully STINKY!

Standing before us was a crystal lake, it was the bluest of blues.

The woods that surrounded the lake were much different than what we had seen in the rest of the woodland.

There was an array of vivid colors and plants of all shapes and sizes.

It was a secret utopia, not known to us before.

"Are we the first to discover this place?" I wondered.

We found no dinosaurs. But we did find adventure, danger, even treasure in this magical place, together.

And that beats yard work any day!

Ralph spoke up softly.

"Are you guys hungry?" he asked.

"YES!" I agreed.

"Wait, what?" Belle agreed too.

Rested and content with our discoveries, we headed for home.

Plus one splinter, minus one shoe, covered in mud, hungry, stinky and with a mysterious bone.

Part Five
Home

Back in the neighborhood, the smell of delicious afternoon barbecue's filled the air. Drowning out the horrible smell of freshly chopped grass, yuck.

Bursting with excitement, we told of our adventures and the secret lake.

Our moms laughed at our stories, and our dads, well, they just talked about the new "HEDGE MUNCHER 9000!"

...Typical...

We never did find out what type of bone we had found. But that's okay because it is still pretty cool no matter what kind it is (a dinosaur).

I got to keep the bone.

Ralph didn't want anything to do with the bone.

" Nooo WAY!" he said...Scaredy cat...

Belle thought I should keep the bone also, and maybe one day find out what type it is (a dinosaur).
I guess Belle found enough dead bugs to keep her busy with her collection.

Ralph, Belle and I go to the secret lake almost every Saturday, you know, that whole yard work thing.

As it turns out, Ralph found a short cut through the woods, so now it only takes like five minutes to get there...

CAN you believe THAT?!

For Lily, Isabel and Patrick, always choose adventure.

For more information contact: youhaveawildimagination. com

Summary: To avoid a Saturday filled with yard work, Lizzy takes to the woods in search of adventure.

ISBN: 978-0-9995804-1-7

[1. Juvenile Fiction/Action and Adventure/General]
[2. Juvenile Fiction/Humorous Stories]
[3. Juvenile Fiction/Readers/Beginner]